T0197540

The Enchanted Forest

Story & Illustrations
by Gail Bellucci

To order additional copies of this book, contact:
Xlibris
844-714-8691
www.Xlibris.com
Orders@Xlibris.com

ISBN: Softcover   978-1-6698-4832-5
         Hardcover   978-1-6698-4833-2
         EBook   978-1-6698-4831-8

Library of Congress Control Number: 2022917702

Print information available on the last page

Rev. date: 11/03/2022

The Enchanted Forest

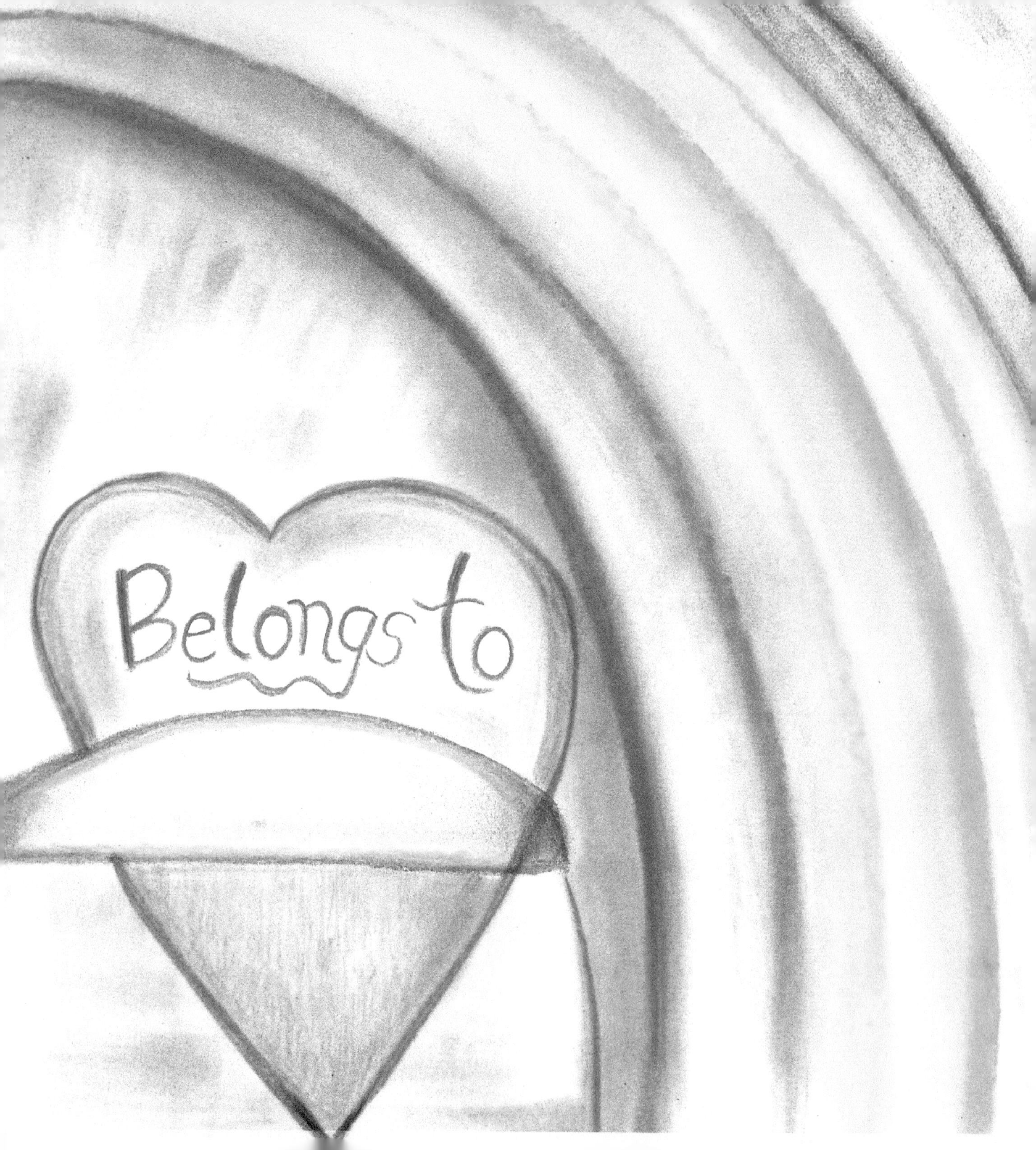
Belongs to

Acknowledgments

Open a new window into your
world, use your imagination,
and read fairy tales.

Many thanks to James, my son,
who photographed my canvas rug.

3

*T*here once was an Enchanted Forest deep in a magical place. A magical lady and her three helpers ran the forest. They would come every day to see everyone who lived there. All of the animals could see them and hear them coming! She was a magical lady named Blossom who grew beautiful flowers on her head. They smelled like lavender. Behind her were her helpers: Ariel, Athena, and Aura. They follow her every day to the forest to help everyone.

IT WAS MAGICAL!!!!!

*L*et's start with the friends in the forest.

The first place they went was called "The Hill." The insects who lived there would tunnel all day looking for worms and grubs to eat. Blossom would call out to them, "Oh, are you on your flowers?" They replied, "Yes, we are exhausted from looking for food. We are taking a nap. Are you checking up on us?" "Yes," replied Blossom.

"Ok," replied Red the insect, sitting on his throne with his friend called Human Face. "We will talk to you soon."

Blossom and her helpers came to check on her friends in the forest. "My, these flowers are beautiful! I brought my magical bird, Apollo, with me. He is on his way to check up on his friends playing in the rainbow. He will stop any arguments with the other birds. We have to get going now. We will be on our way."

All of a sudden, Blossom heard, "aye, aye, aye," and thought, "What is that making all that racket?" They heard, "I am stuck between these vines! Can you help me?"

"Of course, my helpers will pull the vines away," said Blossom. "Thank you very much," replied Mellow. "They grow overnight and I get stuck in them every evening between these mammoth flowers." They were so glad he was OK. "They call me Mellow Yellow because of my skin."

$\mathcal{M}$eanwhile, Blossom and her helpers saw the Whirly Boy and Abe, the Ape, playing in the vines. Blossom yelled, "What are you doing up there?" "We are hanging and swinging and playing hide and seek. These vines are so much fun!"

*T*hen they ran into Wiggly Eyes. He was enjoying playing and acting like the vines were a slippery slope. He was slipping and sliding.

All the animals were excited to see the rainbow. It was hard to find everyone, but they could see some of the friends that were hiding and playing in the rainbow.

There were so many vines along the way, as Blossom and her helpers approached them. They saw a caterpillar named Blue. He was climbing up to see the rainbow.

All of a sudden, we hear the Sun yelling at Blue. "Hey up there," the Sun said, "please hurry up. I want to see the rainbow. I am rising, so please keep moving." "OK, OK," screamed the blue caterpillar. "I am almost there."

As he climbed, he saw the dancing doves swinging through the vines. What a sight!!!!!

*I*n the enchanted forest, there was a rainbow every day.

Everyone was flapping their wings in frenzy. They got so excited to see the RAINBOW!

There was a flurry of activity. The birds were chirping in excitement to see all the colors of the rainbow.

A large bird, Striker, sticking his head through the rainbow, was watching the other sun, staring at him. Now the rainbow was getting brighter and brighter. More animals were coming to see the rainbow.

*E*veryone wanted to swing in the most beautiful rainbow ever!!!

Crazy bird was trying to bite a bubble ball while looking at Mr. Batwing. "Hey, let others have fun too. Share the rainbow," said Mr. Batwing.

They looked up and viewed the rainbows they slid downwards, toward the ground, to let other flowers, insects, and humans enjoy the festival of color in the rainbow.

REMEMBER, we all should try to get along with each other.

A lesson learned, when you meet someone along your travels, friends you have met.

Always be polite and courteous.

Helping your friends will always make you feel good, and they will thank you too!!!

You never know in life when you might come across an event, or a phenomenon that is truly a wonderful observation, A RAINBOW.

When you look at the Enchanted Rug, what do you see?

Are some characters hiding?

Can you find the missing characters not mentioned in my story?

You can write about them, give them a name, and you can imagine the unknown ones into your own story.

*H*ere are some fun facts about rainbows:

Did you know there are different types of rainbows?

1. A fogbow is a type of rainbow that occurs when fog or a small cloud experiences sunlight through them. The colors are usually white, blue, and red.

2. Moon bows, or lunar rainbows, usually are formed by tiny droplets of water, often from a rain cloud or a waterfall.

3. What are the seven colors of the rainbow? The spectrum in order contains, red, orange, yellow, green, blue, indigo, and violet. Use ROYGBIV to remember.

4. A rainbow has to have rain and light. Rain droplets and the sun have to be out. This occurs when light hits the water droplets with white light creating colors of the rainbow. Most rainbows have an arc in the sky.

*S*o when you see a rainbow remember, it is a sight of white light that changes your eyes and creates an optical illusion through the spectrum of colors.

Hope you have enjoyed the
"Enchanted Forest"
and learning facts about rainbows.

Printed in the United States
by Baker & Taylor Publisher Services